Kung Fu
Kitties

No part of this publication may be reproduced in whole or in part, or stored in a retrieval system, or transmitted in any form or by any means, electronic, mechanical, photocopying, recording, or otherwise, without written permission of the publisher. For information regarding permission, write to Sigil Publishing, Box 824, Leland, Michigan 49654.

ISBN 0-9785642-8-5

Printed in the U.S.A.

First Printing, December 2010

Kids, Cats, or Rats ...

Who Committed the Purrfect Crime?

Lincoln Township Public Library
2099 W. John Beers Rd.
Stevensville, MI 49127
(269) 429-9575

CONTENTS

Real Heroes Read!

realheroesread.com

#11: Kung Fu Kitties

David Anthony
and
Charles David Clasman

Illustrations
Lys Blakeslee

Traverse City, MI

Home of the Heroes

abigail

andrew

zoë

CHAPTER 1:
MEET THE HEROES

Welcome to Traverse City, Michigan, population 18,000. The city has everything you might expect: malls, movie theaters, schools, and playgrounds. Kids swim here in the summer and build snowmen during the winter. Sometimes they pretend that they live in an ordinary place.

But Traverse City is far from ordinary. It is set on one of the Great Lakes and attracts tourists in every season. Thousands of people visit every year.

Still, few of them know the city's real secret. Even fewer talk about it. You see, Traverse City is home to three keen superheroes. This story is about them.

Meet Abigail, the oldest of our heroes by a whole eight minutes. When it comes to sports, she can't be beat—not at kickball, not at kayaking, and certainly not at kneeboarding. After earning a black belt, she took karate to the next level. Now she can catch flies with her chopsticks. Pop flies in the outfield, that is.

Andrew comes next. He's Abigail's twin brother, younger by a measly eight minutes. If it has wheels, Andrew can ride it. He's killer, kickin', and the king on wheels. Just watch him roll in karate class. He doesn't chop the usual boards and blocks. He breaks steel beams with his bean!

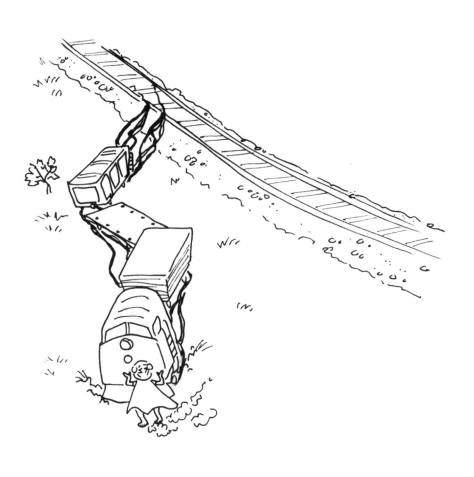

Last but definitely not least is Baby Zoë. She's proof that big things can come in small packages. She still wears a diaper, but she can stop a runaway train in her bare feet. She puts the *kid* in *skids*.

Together these three heroes keep the streets and neighborhoods of Traverse City, Michigan, and America safe. Together they are …

CHAPTER 2:
MEET THE KITTIES

"Kitties!" Zoë exclaimed, fidgeting on the family room floor. Her favorite TV show, *Kung Fu Kitties*, was about to start.

"The popcorn is on me," Andrew said, rolling into the room on his Heelies. He meant it, too. Literally. A big bowl of buttery popcorn was balanced on his head.

"I've got drinks," Abigail said. She dashed into the room behind Andrew, digging into her duffel bag.

Drinks, however, wasn't exactly what she meant. She had a drink. *One* DRINK. It was a tall orange cooler filled with sports juice like the kind kept on the sidelines at a football game. Sometimes the team dumped the drink onto their coach's head after a big win.

"Killjoys!" Zoë shushed her siblings. The twins were doing too much talking and not enough watching. The Kung Fu Kitties was about to begin.

Gong!

That's how the show started every week, with the crash of a gong. Mr. Meowee appeared on screen first. He was the Kung Fu Kitties' teacher. No one knew exactly how old he was, but Mr. Meowee had been hunting mice since before the invention of the mousetrap. Practice makes *purrrr*fect he often told his students.

Gong!

The first of Mr. Meowee's three students needed the most reminding. Moose Lee was as lazy as a cat in a patch of sunshine and almost as big as his name. Next to kung fu, his favorite thing to do was eat. He ate sardines in his sleep, poultry at practice, and tuna at the tournament. Moose Lee put the *eat* in *defeat.*

Gong!

The second student, Chuck Morris, was Moose Lee's exact opposite. He was pure muscle, solid, and strong. Dogs feared him, and mice fainted at the mention of his name. Chuck Morris put the *cat* in dog*cat*cher.

Gong!

Lucy Mew completed and complemented the trio of kitties. She was a shadow, a stalker, and a spy. Hear her coming? Never. See her? Too late. Lucy Mew made silence seem loud and made darkness her playground. She put the *night* in her enemies' *nightmares*.

In this week's episode, the Kung Fu Kitties battled their archenemy, the Rattler. The Rattler was part rat, part snake, and all venom. He could chase a cat up a tree, steal bones from a hungry dog, and still have to time to try to take over the world. With every diabolical deed, his tail twitched and buzzed like a rattlesnake's.

"Ratical," he often snickered while rubbing his filthy paws together.

For the next 30 minutes, the heroes watched, laughed, and cheered. They enjoyed every episode of *Kung Fu Kitties*, but tonight's episode was special. Why? Because tomorrow the heroes would meet the Kung Fu Kitties in person.

Mr. Meowee was opening a dojo in Traverse City, their hometown! That was a special gym where kung fu was taught. Tomorrow was the grand opening, and the heroes planned on being first in line at the door.

Gong!

CHAPTER 3:
FISTS OF FURRY

"What time is it now?" Andrew asked Abigail. His voice cracked, sounding urgent, but Abigail knew better.

Nevertheless, she glanced at her watch. Her brother wasn't the only impatient one.

"9:52 am," she said. "Three minutes later than the last time you asked."

Andrew groaned and shuffled his feet. Time was moving so slowly! Superheroes should be able to do something about that. How about, time flies when you're wanting none?

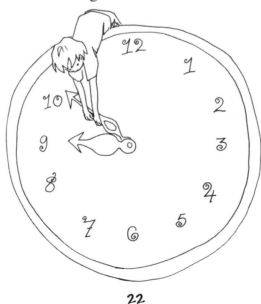

Andrew and his sisters waited in line outside Fists of Furry. That was the new kung fu dojo opening up in town. Almost everyone they knew was there.

"Morning, heroes," Officer Duncan McDoughnut greeted them. "Ready to kung fu?" Then to prove he was, he jumped into a kung fu fighting stance.

The heroes tried hard not to laugh. Officer McDoughnut was their favorite police officer, even if he had clucked like a chicken and tried to make them drink Fowl Mouthwash.*

"Good morning," Abigail and Andrew smiled.

"Keystone," Zoë muttered to herself.

*See Heroes A²Z #6: Fowl Mouthwash

Mr. Meowee appeared at the door eight minutes late. He bowed deeply to the people outside and then turned the lock. The door swung slowly open.

"Greetings and welcome," he said to the crowd. "You are all invited to enter my humble dojo. Please come in."

The crowd cheered and rushed forward. One by one, they filed past Mr. Meowee. Some stopped for pictures or to shake his furry paw. Others bowed quietly before moving on.

Andrew did both and more. He stopped, snapped some shots, shook hands, and asked for a favor.

"Say it," he grinned at the kung fu master. "Please."

Mr. Meowee stared at Andrew in silence. The whole crowd quieted. Abigail worried that her brother had insulted the teacher. How rude to ask a favor so soon!

Finally Mr. Meowee cleared his throat. *"Purrrr*-fect," he purred, his trademark expression. It didn't sound exactly like it did on TV, but it was close.

"Cat-tastic!" Andrew exclaimed. Even Mr. Meowee smiled and bumped fists with Andrew.

A long table stood in the lobby of the dojo. Behind it sat Lucy Mew, Moose Lee, and Chuck Morris—the Kung Fu Kitties! They were there to sign autographs.

The heroes rushed forward. "Kiss?" Zoë asked, her tiny arms spread wide.

Lucy Mew took one look at her and made a sour face. She cleared her throat noisily, then hacked up a hairball next to the table.

"Lucy doesn't kiss babies," she sneered. "Don't you have a dolly?" When Zoë frowned, the other two kitties laughed.

"How about a fist bump, Moose?" Andrew asked. That wasn't as personal as a kiss. Surely the big cat would agree.

Moose Lee folded his thick arms across his chest. "No," he growled in his deep voice. "You're too puny. I would hurt you."

"Hurt me?" Andrew chuckled. "I'm a super-hero like you. I'm Kid Roll. Maybe you've heard of me?"

The large cat snorted. "Heard of you?" he repeated. "I can barely *see* you. You're like a tiny flea. Shoo, tiny flea. Go away."

Abigail grabbed her siblings by the elbows. She had seen and heard enough. The Kung Fu Kitties were *not* the heroic characters they played on TV. They were bullies.

Behind them, Lucy Mew made kissy noises. Moose Lee taunted Andrew:

"The tiny flea is fleeing!"

When the heroes passed Chuck Morris, he pretended to let them go. But at the last moment, he stuck out a foot to trip Abigail.

"See you next fall!" he howled.

So much for the heroes meeting their heroes. What a heroic disappointment!

CHAPTER 4:
KUNG FU CRIMINALS

"Knaves!" Zoë sobbed. She had never felt more disappointed. The Kung Fu Kitties had turned out to be fakes. They were feline phonies!

"There, there," Mom whispered, gently patting Zoë's back.

"Who wants ice cream?" Dad asked. Such an offer usually cheered everyone up.

Not today. Zoë cried harder, and the twins sat down on the curb outside Fists of Furry. It was going to take something other than treats to sweeten then heroes' mood.

Something, it turned out, was the police.

Officer Duncan McDoughnut stormed out of the dojo. His face was dark red, almost purple.

"Those no-good furballs," he grumbled. "They're trouble, I say. I just don't have proof ... yet."

Abigail raised her head. Trouble? Proof? Those sounded like superhero business.

"Can we help, Officer," she asked.

Andrew joined in. "Trouble is my middle name," he said.

"Your first and last, too," Abigail grinned, elbowing him in the ribs.

"Hello, heroes," Officer McDoughnut said. "I'm glad to see you. Did those Kung Fu Kitties seem *strange* to you?"

"They were rude," Andrew frowned.

"Bullies," Abigail said.

"Knuckleheads," Zoë added, finally drying her eyes.

Duncan McDoughnut nodded in agreement. He knelt down and lowered his voice.

"I have a secret," he whispered. "There has been a recent wave of crime across Michigan. I think those cats are responsible."

Mom and Dad gasped, and the heroes leaned in close. Officer McDoughnut continued to nod.

"Even since those cats showed up, milk has been disappearing everywhere," he explained. "Pints have been pilfered in Pentwater. Gallons grabbed in Gaylord. Quarts kidnapped in Quincy. Bottles burglarized in Birmingham. Someone even robbed Moomers the other night."

Now everyone gasped. Moomers! That was the dairy farm in Traverse City where some of the yummiest ice cream was made. It was a local specialty. Delicious!

Andrew and Abigail stood up. They were finished feeling sorry for themselves.

"What can we do to help?" they asked. No
one messed with Moomers.

"I need three deputies that I can trust," Officer McDoughnut said. "I want you to spy on those
cats. Catch them in the act of stealing milk. Get the
proof I need to arrest them."

This time it was the heroes' turn to nod. "We'll
do it," Abigail said. "We'll catch those Kung Fu
Criminals."

CHAPTER 5:
MILK THIEVES

Hours after dark, the heroes prepared to leave. Most of Traverse City was asleep, but the heroes had no time to rest. They were deputies now, crime fighters, and private detectives. Bedtime had been postponed.

"Take these," Mom said, handing each of her children a brown paper sack.

"Midnight snacks," Dad explained. "To keep up your strength."

Without looking inside, the twins knew what their parents had packed: peanuts for Abigail, the kind sold at baseball games; cookies for Andrew, round like wheels; S.U.P.E.R. Baby Formula for Zoë.*

Zoë, however, couldn't help herself. She peeked into her sack using x-ray vision.

*See Heroes A²Z #7: Guitar Rcoket Star

"Thanks, Mom and Dad," Abigail said.

"We'll be careful," Andrew promised.

"Knights," Zoë vowed. The heroes would also be brave and honorable.

Their parents nodded, but didn't say goodbye. "Our babies are growing up," Dad sniffed, wiping a tear from his cheek. "They already work for the police."

"Next they will be running for president," Mom sighed. "Where has the time gone?"

The heroes didn't say goodbye either. They waved and then sped into the city. Fists of Furry was located on Eighth Street. They arrived quickly. Lights shone outside, yet the inside of the dojo was dark. No one seemed to be home.

"Let's roll around back," Andrew suggested. "That's probably where the sneaky stuff takes place."

He was right. Behind the dojo, three figures dressed in black were sneaking silently into the night. The Kung Fu Kitties were on the prowl!

The trio of cats moved like ninjas. They shifted from shadow to shadow along Eighth Street. They darted down US-31. When they reached the Meijer store, the kitties crept quietly behind the long building.

Meijer was huge, like a mall all by itself. Imagine a toy store, grocery store, and a department store in one building. Build that into a store big enough to sell twice as much stuff, and that was Meijer. A little bit of everything and a lot of most. It was founded in Michigan in 1934.

"Did anyone bring a shopping list?" Abigail asked.

Andrew pointed. The Kitties had their list, but it was short. Just one item was on it: milk.

Activity surrounded the loading dock behind Meijer. An 18-wheeler idled in front of the open bay. Two delivery drivers sat back to back on the ground, tied together with yarn. In the cab of the truck sat Lucy Mew. Meanwhile, Moose Lee and Chuck Morris were loading crates of milk into the back.

"Kleptomaniacs!" Zoë gasped. The Kung Fu Kitties really were thieves! They had to be stopped.

CHAPTER 6:
FRAMED!

Andrew held up three fingers and silently counted them down. Three, two, one—go! Then he tiptoed around the corner toward the Kung Fu Kitties. His sisters followed.

"Don't move," he ordered loudly, holding up his deputy's badge. "We've got you surrounded. You're under arrest."

In his mind, he sounded tough and confident. But the Kung Fu Kitties must have heard something else, because Chuck Morris and Moose Lee dropped to their knees. They grabbed their bellies and roared with laughter. Lucy Mew laughed so hard she fell out of the truck.

First the heroes frowned. Then their faces reddened. Didn't the Kung Fu Kitties know who they were? The heroes weren't used to being mocked.

"This isn't a joke," Abigail snapped. "You cats are going to jail."

"Kaput," Zoë said, pretending to dust off her hands. The Kung Fu Kitties were done, finished, over. They just didn't know it yet.

Or maybe they were pretending not to know.

The heroes were still trying to figure out which when Moose Lee attacked. He came at them in a roll, like Andrew but furry and fat. The ground groaned beneath his weight. Watch out for the Feline Flattener!

Wham!

Moose Lee bowled into the heroes like a giant fudge blob on Halloween.* His blubbery belly even blasted Zoë who had been floating above the ground.

*See Heroes A²Z #2: Bowling Over Halloween

The unexpected attack knocked the heroes backward. Moose Lee's bulbous belly packed a punch, not to mention a lot of lunch. Their arms and legs whirling, the heroes tumbled into a waiting Chuck Morris. The muscular cat had dashed behind them while Moose Lee rolled ahead.

Shing-shing! Out popped Chuck Morris's claws. Then left-right-left—three quick slashes caught the heroes and spun them like tops.

Abigail whirled out of control. Her brother twirled, and Zoë curled. 'Round and 'round they spun and unfurled into the trap of the kung fu cat girl.

"*Hyah!*" Lucy Mew shouted. Crouching low, she struck with her tail three times. *Sweep! Sweep! Sweep!* She knocked the heroes clean off their feet.

The male kitties purred with laughter. Nice finish, Lucy Mew. In fact, the beginning and middle of the attack couldn't have gone better for the kitties.

Chuck Morris sneered. "Who named those kids Heroes A^{2}Z? They're more like Zeroes 1^{2}3."

"Kukoo," Zoë muttered, holding her head in her hands. She felt dizzier than if she'd fallen off a merry-go-round. Even the birdies circling her head were seeing stars. Stop the world. She wanted to get off.

Moose Lee held one clawed finger to his lips and a cell phone to his ear.

"Hush, zero," he scolded Zoë. "I'm making an important call." Then his face brightened. "Hello, police? I want to report a robbery. I've caught the thieves who have been stealing milk. You won't believe who it is …"

The heroes' mouths fell open as one. At once, they knew what was happening. The Kung Fu Kitties were trying to frame them for the robberies!

CHAPTER 7:
GOT HANDCUFFS?

"You won't get away with this," Abigail said. She and her siblings had been whipped and tripped by the Kung Fu Kitties. Now they were too dizzy to stand.

They were also too dizzy to prevent what happened next. Moose Lee twisted open a gallon of milk. He turned it upside down and poured the whole jug on the heroes' heads.

"Hey!" Andrew sputtered.

"What's the big idea?" Abigail complained.

Moose Lee hissed with laughter. "No use crying over spilled milk," he snickered.

"Or when a bully steals your lunch," Lucy Mew added, and she did just that. She snatched the heroes' snacks and replaced them with pints of milk.

Before the heroes could react, sirens shrieked into range. Blue and red lights flashed. Tires squealed to a stop. The police had finally arrived.

"Over here!" Abigail called, glad to spot a familiar face.

Officer Duncan McDoughnut burst from his squad car. He clutched a pair of handcuffs in both hands.

"Nobody move," he ordered. "And keep your mouths shut!"

Naturally the heroes did as they were told. They always tried to obey the police. The Kung Fu Kitties, however, weren't listening.

"Here are the real thieves," Chuck Morris said. He jabbed a furry paw at the heroes, pointing. "Look at them. They're covered in milk."

"Check their lunch bags, too," Lucy Mew offered. "I think you'll find more milk in them."

Moose Lee chuckled, "We finally found who's got milk."

got handcuffs?

Chuck Morris strutted forward next. He smiled like the Cheshire Cat and carried a photograph in his paws.

"Look at this, officers," he purred to the police. "It's all the evidence you will need."

Duncan McDoughnut gasped when he saw the photograph. His mouth, eyes, and mustache drooped. He couldn't believe what he was seeing, but he couldn't not believe it either.

Before he spoke, the heroes knew the truth. The photograph was supposed to be of them.

"Growing kids can drink a lot of milk," Officer McDoughnut's partner said. "Superpowered kids must need even more. We probably should have seen this coming."

Officer McDoughnut nodded, looking genuinely disappointed. He had written Andrew up for speeding,* but never anything more serious.

"Arrest them," he said slowly. "And take them downtown."

What a tragedy! Heroes A2Z had turned to crime.

CHAPTER 8: JAILBIRDS

Most jails could not hold the heroes. Zoë could break cell bars with her strength, and Abigail could do the same with a hockey stick. But the Traverse City jail was ready for them.

Recently the heroes had been cloned and their powers given to Veggie Villains.* In case something like that happened again, Duncan McDoughnut had made special modifications to three cells in his jail. The cells could keep clones—or the real heroes—locked up tight.

*See Heroes A²Z #9: Ivy League All-Stars

FAILURE

First, Officer McDoughnut took away Abigail's duffle bag. Without sports equipment, she was almost powerless, like Ironman without his suit.

Next, he locked her in a cell decorated with posters of professional athletes. Sounds perfect for Abigail, right? Wrong. The posters depicted famous sports stars that had never won the big game. They were the opposite of Abigail, anti-champions.

Her brother's cell could be described in one word: square. There was nothing round, circular, or even oval anywhere in or near it. The police sat Andrew on a square bed. They fed him bread and water on a square plate and in a square cup. They gave him a baby's square building blocks to play with.

Never before had Andrew felt so hopeless or square. There was no wheeling his way out of this one.

Zoë's cell had a simple design. No bars or furniture, just a steel door with a tiny window. Under most circumstances, such a door wouldn't be enough to keep Zoë in. She could smash it, melt it with her lasers, or use any number of awesome superpowers to escape.

Today, however, the door could have been made of glass. She wouldn't hurt it no matter what.

On the back of the door, you see, was something special: a poster of her parents. Nothing would make her damage that!

All three heroes were stuck. Trapped! They couldn't escape and they couldn't believe where they were in: *Jail!* Only criminals were supposed to be put in jail. In fact, the heroes had helped arrest one of the prisoners in a nearby cell. Zoë heard him speak first.

"So who has pie on her face now?" a familiar voice teased.

Zoë cringed. She knew that voice. It belonged to one of the heroes' archvillains.

But who?

CHAPTER 9:
CRY ME A RIVER

Across the hall from Zoë, a man clutched the bars to his cell. He wore an army uniform and a red helmet with a long stem. He also laughed nonstop like a madman.

Zoë frowned at him. His name was General Chaos. She knew him well. He was obsessed with everything cherry—pies, pits, candy coating, and bombs. He had even tried to cover Michigan in cherry trees.* Stopping him hadn't been easy.

*See Heroes A²Z #3: Cherry Bomb Squad

"Baby Zoë!" General Chaos giggled. Talking wasn't easy for him. He couldn't stop laughing. "I never expected to see you he-he-here."

Zoë didn't reply. She turned her back and folded her arms. General Chaos was a bully. She wasn't interested in anything he had to say.

"You're har-har-hardly perfect," the general continued, still chuckling. "Superheroes are supposed to wear costumes, not dirty diapers." He went on and on, becoming meaner and meaner.

Zoë tried not to listen. She plugged her ears. She hummed. She stomped her feet. Nothing worked. Having superhero hearing wasn't always a blessing.

Finally she couldn't take it anymore. General Chaos wouldn't quit. She sat on the floor, hung her head, and a single tear dripped from her eye. *Plip!*

General Chaos heard it and cackled with glee. "Cry me-hee-hee a river!" he shrilled. "Some hee-hee-hero you are!"

That was it. The crack that broke the dam. Zoë couldn't hold back any longer. She burst into tears.

Now when most babies cry, they can make quite a fuss. They can kick and scream. They can turn red and turn on their faucet. Zoë was no exception. Today she simply skipped directly to the last step.

Waaaaaaaah!

She cried like no baby had cried before. And the more she cried, the deeper her pool of tears became.

Deeper ...

And deeper …

And deeper … until her cell was full and she was swimming in her tears. In fact, the water rose so high that it leaked out the window of Zoë's cell.

Officer Duncan McDoughnut noticed immediately. "Zoë?" he inquired. "Did you have an accident?"

For all her powers, Zoë was still a baby in a diaper. He charged down the hall and unlocked her door.

Whoosh!

A tidal wave of tears blasted the policeman when he opened the door. He tumbled in a rush like a surfer knocked off his board.

"Kick!" Zoë shouted, meaning "swim, stay afloat." She caught the officer's collar and held on.

The current carried them down the hall. They bumped and bobbed and finally burst into an empty cell.

Splash!

Their wild, wet ride ended against a wall.

"Are you alright?" Officer McDoughnut asked. He may have had to arrest Zoë, but that didn't mean he disliked her.

She shrugged. "Kinda," she replied, hating what she was about to do. Her body felt fine, just wet, but her heart hurt.

Slam!

Before the officer knew what was happening, Zoë had slipped out of the cell. She slammed the bars shut behind her, locking him inside. She was free, but Officer McDoughnut was not.

Had Zoë really turned into a criminal?

CHAPTER 10:
CHEESE-IN-EASE

"Let me out, Zoë," Officer McDoughnut said, forcing a smile. The policeman was locked in one of his own jail cells. Zoë had trapped him there.

Nearby, General Chaos cackled, "Don't listen to him, kid. Set me free-hee-hee."

Zoë shook her head and raised her arms. "Keep," she told them, as in "keep tight, keep safe, and keep quiet." The pair was exactly where Zoë needed them: out of the way for now.

Zoë turned to her siblings who were also be-hind bars. "Keys?" she asked.

Abigail pointed to a peg on the wall outside her cell. A key ring hung from it. "There," she said. "Just like in the Old West."

"Yeah," Andrew grinned from the next cell. "Only high-tech."

The keys, you see, weren't metal. They were plastic keycards with magnetic strips like credit cards. If this was the Old West, Zoë was a cowgirl from the future.

Minutes later, Zoë and her siblings were free. They did not, however, release General Chaos or Duncan McDoughnut.

"We'll come back for you," Abigail promised the policeman. "We're still heroes. You'll see."

"What about me-hee-hee?" General Chaos interjected.

Andrew shook his head. "You-who-who can boo-hoo-hoo. You're staying put for another three to five years."

"Karma," Zoë nodded. Sometimes the bad guys got exactly what they deserved.

"You're not supposed to leave," Officer McDoughnut said. "Where do you think you're going?"

"Fists of Furry," Andrew and Abigail answered. They would return not to the scene of the crime. They would go where the criminals could be seen.

Traveling by rooftop was the quickest route. Abigail vaulted from building to building. Zoë flew and Andrew caught a ride on her cape.

The Fists of Furry dojo came into view quickly.
So did a black and white tanker truck painted like a
spotted cow.

"That's a milk truck," Andrew observed.

Abigail nodded. "And that's a hose leading
into the dojo. Look!"

Sure enough, a thick hose snaked its way from
the truck to the dojo. It disappeared into an open
basement window.

"Keepsake?" Zoë wondered, scratching her
head. The Kung Fu Kitties weren't just stealing
milk. They were pumping it into their dojo. The
question was, why?

The heroes huddled around the basement window. Red and orange lights pulsed within. They blinked on the control panel of a strange machine. The machine was shaped like a milk jug with a hose plugged into its top. Black letters on the machine's face spelled the words:

CHEESE-IN-EASE

"Cheese?" Andrew murmured. "Why would cats make cheese?"

Abigail tapped her brother on the shoulder and pointed. "That's why," she said.

Farther in the basement was a frightening sight. Row upon row of mechanical mice stood stiffly at attention like soldiers.

"Rat robots!" Andrew exclaimed.

Yes, rats, not mice, though the distinction didn't settle anything. Rats, mice—both made as much sense as cheese. Why would either be at a feline dojo?

"Knob," Zoë said, reaching for the dojo's backdoor. She and her siblings could wonder all night, but going inside would be the easiest way to find answers.

Not that the heroes expected to find easy answers inside the dojo. They expected the Kung Fu Kitties. They expected a fight. What they got, though, was a surprise.

"Mee-yow!"

Just inside the dojo's back entrance stood four cages. The cages were large enough to hold 100-pound Labrador retrievers, but that wasn't what was inside them today.

The Kung Fu Kitties and Mr. Meowee were locked inside!

"Help up!" they pleaded. "Please. Let us out!"

CHAPTER 11:
CATNIP WHIP

The heroes stared at the Kung Fu Kitties, and the Kung Fu Kitties stared back. The only difference? The Kitties were in cages. No sound disturbed the silence of the dojo. Not the swish of a whisker. Not the twitch of a tail. The phrase "Cat got your tongue?" had never seemed more fitting.

Finally Abigail broke the silence. She couldn't believe the Kung Fu Kitties were really prisoners. "Is this a trick?" she demanded, hands on her hips.

"Why should we trust you?" Andrew added.

Of course the twins wanted to believe in the Kung Fu Kitties. Until recently, the Kitties had been the heroes' heroes.

Mr. Meowee backed up and bowed to the heroes. "Please forgive us," he said humbly. "We were not your enemies on *purr*pose."

He sounded sincere, but something cut him off. His yellow eyes widened, and he pointed urgently with a paw. "Behind you!" he hissed.

Andrew snorted. *"Riiiight!* There's someone behind us. That joke is flatter than a popped tire."

No sooner had he spoken than a new sound filled the dojo. It was a sound he and the others knew well. It was the sound of a rattle.

The Kung Fu Kitties hissed and flexed their claws. Their fur bristled and stood on end. Even before the heroes spun around, they knew who was behind them.

The Rattler! The Kung Fu Kitties' arch-enemy.

"Down, Kitties!" the Rattler snarled. "My catnip whip will make you obey!"

Crack!

"No, not the whip!" the Kitties cried. But it was already too late. Their eyes were starting to glaze, and their shoulders sagged. Another crack of the whip would completely hypnotize them.

Crack!

The Kung Fu Kitties lost all their fight. They slumped to the floor like sleepy kittens with bellies full of milk. *Purr,* was all they said.

The heroes were on their own against the Rattler.

CHAPTER 12:
KIDS VS. KITTIES

Suddenly everything made sense. Why the Kung Fu Kitties had been behaving like villains. Why cheese was being made in the dojo's basement.

The Rattler was behind it all—he and his catnip whip.

"Time to come out and play, Kitties," he howled, snapping the whip over his head.

Crack! And just like that, the doors to the four cat cages opened. The catnip whip had power over them, too.

The Kung Fu Kitties clambered out of their cages. Gone were the sleepy looks in their eyes. Now their ears lay flat and their claws were fully extended. The Kitties were ready for a fight.

So, too, were the heroes.

"Attack!" the Rattler shrieked. "Treat the humans like mice!"

Abigail clashed with Lucy Mew, hockey stick in hand like a fighting staff. Block! Parry! Deflect! Neither she nor the kitty could gain an advantage.

Andrew and Chuck Morris met like two tornados. Leg sweep followed roundhouse kick, but nothing connected. Chuck Morris was too fast, and no rolling kung fu could hurt Andrew when he was ready for it.

Only Baby Zoë and Moose Lee connected, and they connected enough for everyone. Too much, in fact.

The pair collided in the middle of the dojo. Baby vs. bully, belly on belly. *Boing!*

Fat cat and baby went flying back they way they came. Imagine two wrecking balls on the loose. Moose Lee smashed through the cat cages and into the wall, creating a moose-sized window. Zoë missed the front door by inches and punched another exit in the shape of her body. Free air conditioning for everyone!

The dojo went silent again. The heroes and the Kitties stopped sparring. The Rattler lowered his whip.

Then a new sound broke the peace. But not a rattle this time. Not more fighting. It was the sound of everything falling apart.

For real.

CRASH!

The walls shook. The floor buckled. The ceiling started to collapse.

"Get down!" someone screamed, and then everything went black.

CHAPTER 13:
FOLLOW THE CHEESE

Fists of Furry was flattened. Not much of the dojo remained standing. Certainly no one inside, not even the nimble Kung Fu Kitties.

Baby Zoë dug herself free of the rubble first. "Kin?" she asked, wondering if her siblings could hear her.

Pop! Pop-pop!

Someone could. First Lucy Mew then Andrew popped out of the debris like prairie dogs out of their dens. Mr. Meowee, Abigail, and the remaining Kung Fu Kitties followed shortly thereafter.

Pop-pop! Pop!

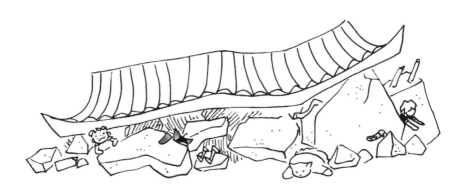

The sleepy look was gone from the Kitties' eyes. The collapse of the dojo must have knocked the sense back into them. They were themselves again.

"Where did the Rattler go?" Andrew wondered. No sign of the villain or his rat robots remained. He and his mechanical army were on the march.

"Maybe he's going to Pinconning?" Abigail suggested, naming a city on Michigan's east coast. It was also known as the Cheese Capital of Michigan. If that Rattler wanted more cheese, Pinconning was the place to go.

"What about Wisconsin?" Andrew asked.

Talk about being famous for cheese! The state to Michigan's left produced over 600 different kinds of cheese. The people who lived there often called themselves cheeseheads. Some of them even wore cheese-shaped hats to football games.

Mr. Meowee made the third and best suggestion. He silently gazed into the night sky and nodded at the full moon.

The heroes' jaws dropped. No wonder Mr. Meowee was the teacher. Without a word, he'd should them where the Rattler wanted to go. To the moon. Nowhere looked more like a big chunk of cheese.

Now all they had to do was figure out how. How did the Rattler plan to get to the moon?

"Kawasaki?" Zoë said, but a motorcycle didn't seem very likely.

"A catapult?" Chuck Morris suggested. Get it? A *cat*apult. Of course a kitty would think that sounded like a good idea.

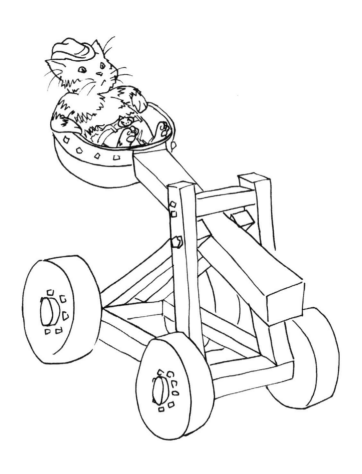

Abigail shook her head. "The Rattler needs parts to build a rocket to reach the moon," she said. "And the best place to find those in Michigan is the Air Zoo."

The Air Zoo, of course! Located in Kalamazoo, Michigan, it was home to over 50 different aircraft. It also had amusement park rides, flight simulators, a zero gravity ride, and more. The Rattler could use the aircraft at the Zoo to build his own rocket.

So the heroes and the Kung Fu Kitties piled into the Catmobile. And why not? Batman had the Batmobile. It made sense that the Kitties would have a Catmobile.

In no time they were speeding south. Air Zoo, here they come!

CHAPTER 14:
WHISKER WAGON TOUR

The Rattler had a special vehicle of his own: the Whisker Wagon. In it, he zoomed across and up and down Michigan. All the while, he played on a flute like the Pied Piper. Every rat that heard the Rattler's music came to join his army.

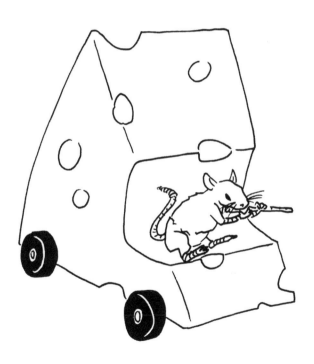

The Rattler tooted his flute in Trout Lake …

He whistled down Whitehall Road past
Michigan's Adventure …

He piped in Pontiac …

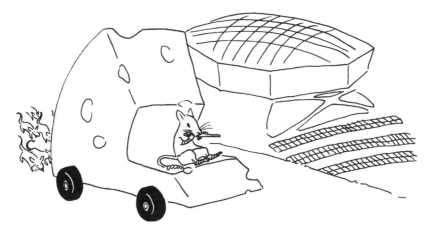

And he fluted past Ferris State University, home of the Bulldogs.

The Rattler's army grew and grew. A couple of rats formed into a few. A few developed into a dozen. A dozen swelled into a score. And a score heaped into a herd. Before long, the rats became too many to count. They were a dark swarm scuttling over the state.

So when the massive militia marched into Kalamazoo, nothing could stop it. Not the heroes who were still far behind. Not even the Michigan National Guard.

Tanks toppled beneath the militia's might. Armed vehicles vamoosed. Soldiers surrendered. None of them could withstand the army's secret weapon:

Cheese breath—stinky, smelly cheese breath. The rodent regiment rolled over the National Guard and arrived at the Air Zoo. The moon shone brightly overhead, waiting.

CHAPTER 15:
TRIPLE KICK

"Kowabunga!" Zoë exclaimed, pointing straight ahead.

Her siblings and the Kung Fu Kitties nodded. They saw what Zoë saw. The parking lot outside the Air Zoo was completely full. Not one free space remained. But instead of cars and buses, the lot was packed with rats, robots, and a rocket.

The Rattler really was headed to the moon. The heroes were almost too late!

In fact, the Rattler stood on top of the rocket now. He held his catnip whip above his head.

"You heroes are outnumbered!" he sneered.

"And the Kung Fu Kitties will still obey me!"

He brought his arm down with a quick snap. *Crack!* went his whip.

The sound of the catnip whip affected the Kitties instantly. Their eyes glazed again. They slumped in their seats. Like back in the dojo, another crack would completely hypnotize them.

If Zoë didn't do something first, that is.

She soared out of the Catmobile straight into the sky with her eyes on the whip. *Z-z-zap!* She squinted, and lasers beamed from her eyes. They blazed into the whip, burning it to ash.

The Kung Fu Kitties would not be hypnotized again.

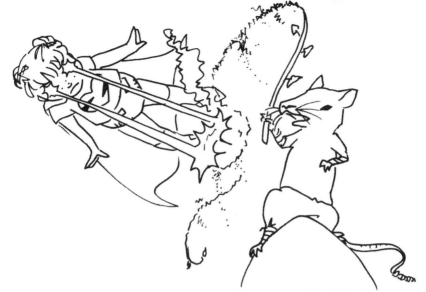

With a snarl, the Rattler tossed aside the remains of his whip. Goodbye, catnip. Hello, rat nip. He drew his flute and blasted a long, shrill note.

Toot!

His robot army came suddenly to life. Each unit snapped its mechanical jaws and started to march.

The heroes and their feline friends were out-numbered twenty-to-one. What terrible odds! How unfair! The Rattler and his robots didn't stand a chance.

"*Purr*form the Triple Kick!" Mr. Meowee commanded, and his Kitties sprang immediately into action.

The first of the three special kicks came from the foot of Chuck Morris. He led with his famous Cowboy Crunch. Yee-haw! One ten-gallon hat required.

Lucy Mew followed with both feet. Appropriate for the second kick. She called her attack Kickity-splits, and the move gave the robots fits.

To complete the Triple Kick, Moose Lee kicked the can—his own can, that is, which sent him bowling into the ranks of the hapless robots. Strike!

"That's the way to whirl!" Andrew cheered. Moose Lee's attack inspired him. How round and like a wheel! Two could play at that game, and did.

Andrew rolled into the fight, rockin' roundhouse kicks with all his might.

Zoë attacked next from above. Her flying kick showed no love.

Abigail finished the footed assault. Like a last-second, game-winning score, her Field Goal Kick put the robots to shame.

Unfortunately, this game was going into over-time.

Blast!

Off!

Spewing smoke and the scent of Swiss, the Rattler's rocket blasted into the sky. The Kung Fu Kitties and the heroes had done their best. But the villain was still escaping.

CHAPTER 16:
CAT-APULT

Up, up, and away. The Rattler's rocket climbed steadily higher. With it went the villain and his cheesy plans for the moon.

Abigail scowled and quickly turned to Zoë. "Time for Sister Shot Put," she said. "We've got a rocket to stop."

"Killer," Zoë grinned, liking the idea. She scrambled onto her sister's shoulder, and then Abigail took over.

"Here …" Abigail began, planting her feet firmly on the ground.

"We …" she scooped Zoë into her right hand. "Go!"

She heaved with all her athletic might, tossing Zoë into the air like a shot put.

Zoë could fly on her own. She did it all the time. But she'd never flown like this before. Never quite so fast.

Whoosh! went the Rattler's rocket. Double *whoosh* went Zoë in pursuit.

She caught the rocket in a blink. A second later she passed it. Then she doubled back around and threw her weight against its nosecone.

A mighty struggle followed in the air. Zoë pushed. The rocket shoved. But neither moved an inch. The pair hung in the sky like figures in a painting.

"Tie game!" Abigail exclaimed, realizing Zoë needed help. "Let's force that rocket into sudden death."

But how, she wondered. She couldn't fly and neither could Andrew. As for the Kung Fu Kitties, getting them off the ground would take …

A catapult!

That was it! Suddenly Chuck Morris's earlier idea didn't seem so crazy.

The twins and the Kitties worked quickly. They didn't know how long Zoë could hold the rocket in place.

Andrew borrowed one of the tires from a nearby P-40 Warhawk, once used in World War II. He wheeled the huge object to where Abigail requested without any trouble. Kid Roll to the rescue.

The Kung Fu Kitties then borrowed a wing from the same aircraft.

Abigail told them where and how to place the parts. She even showed Moose Lee where to sit. Then she stepped back, studied the arrangement, and nodded. It looked good. Ready.

"Start climbing," she instructed everyone else, pointing to a nearby aircraft. For her plan to work, the kitties and kids needed to be in position, too.

Then they needed to jump?

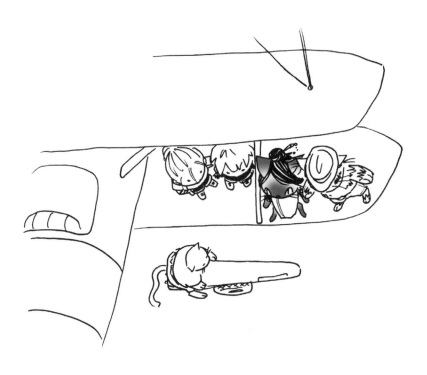

"It's a teeter-totter!" Andrew observed. "But I don't think Moose Lee is having any fun sitting on it yet."

Abigail nodded. "That's right," she agreed. "Don't think. Just jump." Then she shoved her brother into the Kung Fu Kitties.

Hiss! Scream! "Look out below!"

Andrew and the Kitties fell. Abigail jumped with them. Together they dropped onto the empty seat of the giant teeter-totter.

Moose Lee tried to protest. His emerald eyes grew wide, and his mouth fell open. But it was too late to stop what was happening. Too late for the fat cat to even stand.

Andrew, Abigail, and the Kitties hit the teeter-totter at the same time. Their side teetered down. Moose Lee's tottered up.

BOING!

The force sent the chubby cat flying. Moose Lee's arms and legs spun. He screeched as if someone had stepped on his tail. But nothing could stop him from soaring through the air. Nothing but the Rattler's rocket.

Incoming!

CHAPTER 17:
RATTLER RATTLESNAKE

CRASH!

Moose Lee collided with the Rattler's rocket. It was belly on boosters in the great blue yonder.

"Catastrophic!" Chuck Morris gasped from the ground.

"Cataclysmic!" hissed Lucy Mew.

"Copy cats," Andrew snickered, thinking the two Kitties were talking the way Zoë did, usually one word at a time.

But at that moment, Zoë wasn't speaking. She was falling, as were the Rattler's rocket and Moose Lee.

CRASH times two. The rocket smashed into the ground, landing sideways and upside-down. Two smaller objects landed on top of it. Poor Zoë and Moose Lee! What goes up really does come down, sometimes sooner than expected.

The Rattler was the first back on his feet. Before anyone else moved, he scampered to the top of the rocket and glared down at the heroes. His tail shook rapidly with anger.

"What have you done?" he shrieked. "First my whip. Now my ship. You're all going to pay!"

As he spoke, his shaking increased so much that he seemed to be in two and sometimes three places at once. His whole body looked *blurry*.

"W-what's happening to him?" Abigail croaked. She and her siblings had watched every episode of Kung Fu Kitties on TV. They had never seen the Rattler blur before.

"He's changing!" Chuck Morris shouted. "Think about it. What is he?"

"A rat," Andrew answered.

"Yes, and what else?"

Andrew glanced at Abigail. "A rattlesnake?" they said together.

"That'*ssss* right!" the Rattler hissed. "Now look upon your de*ss*struction!"

They did, and they wanted to run. A horror loomed before them. The Rattler had grown. *Stretched.* He was more snake than rat now, and at least as long as his rocket.

The giant Rattler laughed, hissing like an eerie wind. His tail rose and its tip twitched with amazing speed. The heroes could barely look away. The sight was astounding!

The Kung Fu Kitties, however, weren't so lucky. The twitching tail mesmerized them. They watched it, frozen, the way they would watch a ball of yarn rolling across the floor. They were helpless and under its spell. No cat could resist.

Then the Rattler attacked. His tail lashed forward more powerfully than his catnip whip.

Smack! Direct hit to the Kung Fu Kitties. Four felines turned into four flying furballs. None of them even tried to move to avoid the blow.

When they landed, the Kitties didn't get up. They were down and out, suffering from RTKO—a Rat Tail Knock-Out. Goodnight!

The Rattler turned slowly to face the heroes. "Your turn," he snarled. "It'*sss* time for u*sss* to play."

"Play?" Abigail cried. "Play time's over. It's time for your nap."

"Yeah, your *rat*nap!" Andrew growled. "Just like a catnap except you won't be sleeping in the sun. You'll be sleeping in jail."

Then the heroes sprang. All three of them leaped onto the Rattler's back like mongooses onto a real snake.

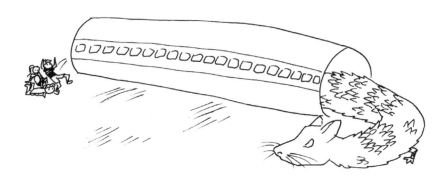

"Brat*sss*!" the Rattled roared. "Get off me!"

Enraged, he thrashed like an angry bronco trying to shake the heroes loose. He snapped his jaws. He flailed his arms. His tail twitched faster than before.

When those failed, he changed tactics. *Wham!* He slammed against a Douglas Skyraider. *Smash!* Then against a Grumman Tomcat.

Still the heroes hung tight. So the Rattler tried again. He slithered through the body of a 727 as if it were a tunnel.

Bonk! Donk! Konk! The close quarters knocked the heroes off, and the Rattler was free. Free and madder than ever.

CHAPTER 18:
RATTRAP

Andrew rolled to his feet and pulled his sisters to theirs. One glance ahead told him all he needed to know. The Rattler was coming back fast.

"Quick!" he shouted. "We need a plan."

Abigail nodded and rummaged through her duffle bag as if it were Santa's sack on Christmas Eve. "Cleats? No. Goalie mask? No. Come on! There has to be something in here that can slow down a rat."

The solution came to Zoë immediately. She snapped her tiny fingers and squealed.

"Kernel!"

Her siblings looked at Zoë in confusion. They didn't understand.

"Do you mean like an army colonel?" Abigail asked. While *kernel* and *colonel* were spelled differently, they were pronounced the same.

"Or a kernel of corn?" tried Andrew.

Zoë smiled and tapped her forehead. "Keen," she said to Andrew.

So he kept trying. "Cornbread? Cornflakes? Corn starch?"

Suddenly Abigail knew. She dropped her bag and sprinted for the edge of town. As she ran, she hollered at the Rattler, "Yoo-hoo, rattrap! Bet you can't catch me!"

The Rattler hissed and changed course. No one insulted him and got away with it! Abigail was first on his hit list now.

Zoë and her brother followed. Andrew kept guessing along the way. "Corn syrup? Corncob pipe? Cornucopia?"

When he and Zoë reached the edge of town, Andrew got his answer. A golden field swayed before him as far as the eye could see. A golden *corn-field*.

But it was not just any cornfield. This field was different. The farmer used it not only to grow crops, but also for a special kind of fun.

"A corn maze!" Andrew exclaimed. "I should have known. A maze is the best placed to trap a rat."

As it sounds, a corn maze is a maze in a cornfield. Pathways run this way and that through the stalks. Some turn, some branch, and some dead-end just like the lines on a paper maze. The difference is that a corn maze is three-dimensional and big enough for people.

In fact, the Rattler proved just that. He dashed into the corn after Abigail and disappeared.

Which is exactly where Andrew and Zoë meant to keep him: disappeared.

"Split up and meet at the exit," Andrew instructed his sister. He had already wheeled around and was zooming toward the city. "And bring cheese!" he called over his shoulder.

But Zoë, too, was moving. She knew the plan, all right. Andrew was just singing the words to someone else's song—hers.

"Karaoke," she muttered. The corn maze had been her idea.

Meanwhile Abigail moved through the maze at top speed. She barely saw the twists and turns before taking them. Sometimes she plowed through the corn like a thresher.

This wasn't about playing by the rules. This wasn't about good sportsmanship. This was about one thing. Outrunning the Rattler.

"You're getting tired," the villain hissed. "*Sss*lowing down. I'll catch you *sss*oon."

He wasn't lying either. Even Abigail had limits. She might be able to win any race, but the Corn Maze Marathon wasn't exactly an Olympic event.

Barely ahead of the Rattler, Abigail burst from the maze. She had found the exit at last. Swaying, golden corn gave way to a braying, grating horn.

Hoonnnkkkk!

Abigail leaped left, barely ahead again. A second later, Andrew rolled into position, behind the wheel of a police wagon. He backed it up to the corn maze.

It was a photo finish! He and the Rattler reached the maze's exit at the same time. Wagon met whiskers, nose to toes.

"Now, Zoë!" Andrew shouted. "Chuck the cheese!"

Faster than a bullet speeding, Zoë soared into view. As she whisked past, she heaved a hunk of Pinconning cheese into the back of the police wagon.

The Rattler saw it. He smelled it. He couldn't resist. He charged out of the maze and into the wagon after the cheese.

Slam!

Once the Rattler was inside the wagon, Abigail threw the doors shut. Her siblings may have started the capture, but she always finished first.

"Enjoy your cheese behind bars," she said.

"Yeah!" Andrew grinned. "Munch mozzarella in a prison cell-a."

Funny, but Abigail thought she could do better. "Try Pinconning's best while you're under arrest."

The twins might have gone on, but the Rattler interrupted them. He flopped onto the floor and bit roughly into his cheese. With his back to the heroes, he snarled at them.

"Hush! I'll eat this Provolone all alone."

Victory! The Rattler was finished. After the heroes repaired the Air Zoo, they could go home.

The same went for the Rattler's army. The rats had wanted cheese, not to operate rodent robots. They helped clean up and then scurried away.

Soon the heroes were back in front of their TV. Popcorn? Check. Cold drinks? Check. Kung Fu Kitties? Triple check. Tonight's episode was special. It starred the Kitties and their new friends Abigail, Andrew, and Baby Zoë.

What a way to thank the heroes. They got to appear on their favorite TV show! Don't forget to set your DVR.